Miss Spider's SUNNY PATCH FRIENDS

All Pupa'ed Out

David Kirk

GROSSET & DUNLAP/CALLAWAY

This book is based on the TV episode "All Pupa'ed Out," written by Nadine Van Der Velde and Scott Kraft, from the animated TV series *Miss Spider's Sunny Patch Friends* on Nick Jr., a Nelvana Limited/Absolute Pictures Limited co-production in association with Callaway Arts & Entertainment, based on the Miss Spider books by David Kirk.

Library of Congress Control Number: 2004019109

ISBN 0-448-43802-X   10 9 8 7 6 5 4 3 2 1

The air in Sunny Patch was sweet with the scent of honeysuckle. In the Cozy Hole, Holley and Miss Spider were baking cookies, when all of a sudden Squirt and Shimmer burst through the door.

"**M**om! Dad! We found a caterpillar," they shouted. "Can we keep her?"

"Caterpillars are a lot of work," Miss Spider told them.

"And they need a lot of feeding," said Holley.

"We promise to take good care of her!" they exclaimed.

"Well, it *would* just be for a little while," Miss Spider said.

"And it would be nice to see one of Mother Nature's most magical moments," Holley added.

Squirt and Shimmer decided to name the caterpillar Cookie.

Cookie was a hungry caterpillar—much hungrier than anyone expected. By the next morning, she had munched through Miss Spider's precious stash of honeysuckle, Dragon's leaf blanket, the kitchen tablecloth, and Holley's favorite slippers.

"Why don't you take Cookie outside for milkweed?" Miss Spider suggested.

In the meadow, things only got worse.

"More, more!" cooed the little caterpillar as she chomped her way through the milkweed.

"Jumpin' June bugs! Taking care of Cookie is much more work than we thought," grumbled Squirt.

The next morning, Cookie wriggled out of bed. She had grown too big for her old skin, so with a *squidgy widgy widge*, she left it dangling.

"Ewwww!" cried Shimmer and Squirt.

A few days later, Miss Spider remarked, "You two look pooped!"

"That caterpillar is always hungry," Squirt moaned.

"And she keeps shedding her icky skin!" complained Shimmer.

It was almost dusk when they realized that nobody had seen Cookie all day.

Suddenly, Holley yelped, "Great buggsy wuggsy! Look at that!"

Dangling from a branch of the Hollow Tree was a golden cocoon.

"That's Cookie!" said Miss Spider with a smile.

"It looks like your job with Cookie is almost done," Miss Spider said. "Now all we have to do is wait."

Squirt and Shimmer helped move the cocoon to the safety of the Cozy Hole.

A few days later the cocoon wiggled and jiggled and twisted and shook. Finally, it split in two! Out came Cookie— a beautiful butterfly.

Everybuggy was amazed. They raced outside to watch Cookie stretch her wings and fly.

"Look at her go!" cried Dragon.

"She's so beautiful," Shimmer sighed.

Soon Cookie returned carrying big bunches of yummy honeysuckle.

"Thanks for taking care of me," she called. "I know I was a lot of work."

"It was worth it," said Squirt. "And thank you for the honeysuckle."

Everybuggy cheered as Cookie and her new friends flew away, their brilliant wings fluttering against the sky.